# TEXAS STAR

by Barbara Hancock Cole

pictures by Barbara Minton

ORCHARD BOOKS · NEW YORK

Orchard Books, A division of Franklin Watts, Inc.
387 Park Avenue South, New York, NY 10016

Manufactured in the United States of America. Printed by General Offset Co., Inc. Bound by Horowitz / Rae.
Book design by Mina Greenstein. The text of this book is set in 18 pt. Cheltenham Oldstyle. The illustrations are
watercolor paintings reproduced in halftone.  10  9  8  7  6  5  4  3  2  1

Library of Congress Cataloging-in-Publication Data
Cole, Barbara Hancock.   Texas star / Barbara Hancock Cole ; illustrated by Barbara Minton.   p.   cm.
"A Richard Jackson book." Summary: Papa grumbles that the family doesn't need another quilt, but is happy to
use it after the quilting bee.   ISBN 0-531-05820-4.   ISBN 0-531-08420-5 (lib. bdg.)
[1. Quilting—Fiction.]  I. Minton, Barbara, ill.  II. Title.  PZ7.C673413Te  1989  [E]—dc19
88-25205  CIP  AC

For Faith and Jerry and Nola,
for Nancy and the memory
of my parents
B.H.C.

To Jeff, Tracy, and Kirsten,
my irrepressible models
B.M.

When the dew in the meadow turned to frost, Mama brought in the begonias from the front porch and hung the get-ready-for-winter list on the kitchen wall.

We raked leaves in our yard and burned them in the field.

Papa put away the scarecrow and turned under the garden with his plow.

And when we had neatly stacked all the winter wood in the shed, Mama said the get-ready-for-winter list was finished. She had checked off every chore. "While we wait for bad weather," she said, "I think I'll have a quilting party."

Papa groaned as if he were about to die.

"Now look here," she said, "nothing could keep you as warm this winter as the Texas Star I'm going to quilt."

Mama gave the orders, and we took the bed apart in the guest bedroom and carried all of it, even the feather mattress, upstairs.

We washed the windows on the inside and the outside and dusted the walls and checked the corners for cobwebs. Then we scrubbed and polished the floor.

"We don't need another quilt," Papa said. "It's too much trouble."
Mama acted as if she didn't hear a word he said. We filled the
wood box and carried the trunk and the rocking chair to the living
room. We dusted the straight chairs on the front porch before we
brought them in.

We did all that work in two days' time. Papa polished and scrubbed and dusted and grumbled and said we didn't need another quilt over and over—at least a hundred times.

When at last we placed the straight chairs around the quilting frames in the front room, Mama said, "Now I have to cook for the quilters."

She made sweet potato pies and shortbread and coconut cake.
Papa cracked the coconut with a hammer and peeled the tough bark
with a sharp knife.

The next morning before the sun came up, the smell of fried chicken and coffee woke us. We got up early because the house was warm, and the cold floor would not shock our feet.

As soon as the frost had melted except in the shadows, Mama's quilting friends arrived.

Once the quilt top and lining had been stretched over the frames, they threaded their needles, and Nancy and I stood close to watch. Silver needles and thimbles flashed, and fingers flew steadily across Mama's Texas Star like small armies marching toward an enemy in the center.

The quilters stopped for shortbread and coffee, and then they stitched again. Stitch. Stitch. Stitch and roll. Stitch. Stitch. Stitch and roll.

They ate the chicken and biscuits, the potato salad and the coconut cake and sweet potato pies. And they stitched and stitched again.

Papa kept wood in the heater and said snow was coming for sure.
By evening the Texas Star was finished, and the quilters went home.

That night snow did come—just as Papa said—
and icy wind blew like a gale.

Papa piled wood on the fire in the fireplace and sat on the floor next to Nancy and me while Mama read to us.

"I've got an idea," Mama said, hurrying from the room when she had read no further than *"Once upon a time..."*

"I guess we did need the Texas Star after all," Papa admitted, his eyes twinkling, as Mama picked up the book to finish our story.